Ruger,
Books are magic!

Alien
Ice
Cream

Ruger,
Real heroes read!

ISBN 978-0-9728461-8-9

Printed in the U.S.A.

Second Printing, July 2008

To

The Captain
#19 Steve Yzerman

Thank you for 22 years.
Enjoy retirement!

CONTENTS

Real Heroes Read!

realheroesread.com

#1: Alien Ice Cream

David Anthony
and
Charles David

Illustrations
Lys Blakeslee

Traverse City, MI

Home of the Heroes

abigail

zoë

andrew

CHAPTER 1:
MEET THE HEROES

Welcome to Traverse City, Michigan, population 18,000. The city has everything you might expect: malls, movie theaters, schools, and playgrounds. Kids swim here in the summer and build snowmen during the winter. Sometimes they pretend that they live in an ordinary place.

But Traverse City is far from ordinary. It is set on one of the Great Lakes and blooms with brilliant colors in the spring. Thousands of people visit every year.

Still, few of them know the city's real secret. Even fewer talk about it. You see, Traverse City is home to three exceptional superheroes. This story is about them.

Meet Abigail, the oldest of our heroes by a whole eight minutes. When it comes to sports, she can't be beat—not at arm wrestling, not at archery, and certainly not at aces on the tennis court. Her duffle bag is stuffed with athletic equipment that never weighs her down. Once she sank a pirate ship with a well-aimed drive of her golf club.

Andrew comes next. He's Abigail's twin brother, younger by a measly eight minutes. If it has wheels, Andrew can ride it. We're talking anything with wheels, no matter the size. From airplanes to automobiles, he is amazing, astounding, and awesome on wheels. He even rode a unicycle to victory in a BMX bike race.

Last but definitely not least is Baby Zoë. She's the strongest of the heroes, like Superman in a diaper. She might not be able to walk that well, but she can fly and shoot lasers from her eyes. Zoë puts the *super* in superhero.

Together these three heroes keep the streets and neighborhoods of Traverse City, Michigan, and America safe. Together they are …

CHAPTER 2:
HOW HOT WAS IT?

"I think I'm going to melt," Andrew complained. He and his sisters were sitting under a sad little limp tree in their front yard. It was the hottest day of the year.

How hot? you ask. Hot enough to fry eggs on the hood of a car.

And that's hot. Gross, but hot.

"Awful," Zoë sighed, dabbing her sweaty forehead with a corner of her cape.

Abigail agreed but she wasn't about to let the heat ruin a summer day. Her superhero's super-brain was always working. Suddenly, she leaped to her feet.

"Slam dunk!" she cried. "I've got it—the swimming pool! C'mon!"

Abigail in the lead, the heroes raced to the pool in the backyard. When they reached it, they stumbled to a stop and their mouths dropped open.

"Abnormal!" Zoë shrieked, staring in horror at the pool.

Abnormal was right. The heat had gotten to the pool. Its water was so hot it was *boiling*. Swimming in there would be worse than taking a bath in a bowl of hot soup.

"This way," Andrew urged, tugging Abigail's elbow. He couldn't let her be the only one to come up with an idea. More importantly, he knew that his idea would be better.

"Who wants to run through the sprinkler first?" he asked with a huge smile. His sisters cheered. Running through the sprinkler would beat the heat!

When Andrew turned on the faucet, the hose coughed and wheezed. Then it spat dust like a mummy's dry sneeze. Not a single drop of water came out.

Seeing her brother sad made Zoë sad too, so she decided to do something. It was time to use her superpowers.

"Artic," she announced, and jumped into the air.

In minutes she flew thousands of miles to the North Pole. There she found a wonderfully chilly and icy iceberg. It was perfect for the scorching day back home.

Flying as fast as she could, Zoë zoomed home with her iceberg. Andrew and Abigail would be so proud! Over Canada, Lake Michigan, and the Sleeping Bear Dunes she sped.

All the while, the temperature rose. Zoë started to sweat and her iceberg started to melt.

Zoë arrived home to discover that the worst had happened. Her wonderfully chilly and icy iceberg had melted! Now it was a tiny cube floating in a tiny puddle in her tiny hand.

"Aww," she sniffed.

How would our heroes ever beat the heat?

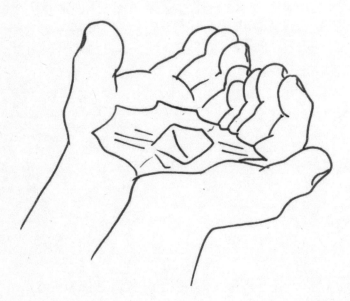

CHAPTER 3:
I SCREAM, YOU SCREAM

Just then, faint music reached our heroes' ears. It was a song they knew, and a song they loved. It was music from an ice cream truck headed their way!

"Ice cream!" the twins shouted. Zoë squealed and forgot about her iceberg.

Sundaes, push-ups, sugar cones, too.
Snow cones, bomb pops—red, white, blue.
I love ice cream, so do you.
I scream, you scream—we all do!

The ice cream song was irresistible. Neighbors from up and down the block shuffled out of their homes, digging for money in pockets, purses, piggy banks, and wallets. Everyone wanted ice cream on a scorching day like this.

Bomb pops, chocolate drumsticks, push-ups, and more. The heroes dreamed of delicious frosty treats, but the ice cream truck remained nowhere in sight.

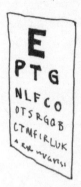

Finally the truck came slowly into view. But it didn't arrive from down the street, and it didn't pull out of a driveway. This truck didn't do those things. In fact, it wasn't like any truck any of them had ever seen before.

"Arrival," Zoë exclaimed, pointing at the sky. Nothing got past her super vision. She could read the fine print on an eye chart blindfolded.

The crowd looked to where Zoë pointed, and the sight caused adults to shriek. Kids cheered, dogs barked, and cats scampered up the trunks of trees.

No one expected to see what they saw. It was impossible, amazing, and couldn't be true.

But they saw it, all of them. They couldn't look away. The ice cream truck floated down from the sky like a spaceship from another world.

CHAPTER 4:
U.F.O. SURE-BURT

"It's not an ice cream truck!" Andrew cheered. "It's an ice cream *spaceship*!"

"Awesome!" his sisters agreed, clapping excitedly.

Sure enough, the ice cream truck was silver and shaped like a flying saucer. Colored lights blinked up and down its surface. On its roof, a long metal antenna crackled with electricity.

Everyone fell silent as the ice cream spaceship descended. When it neared the ground, landing gear like a giant-sized unicycle popped from its under-side. Andrew saw this and grinned.

"If it has wheels, I can ride it," he boasted.

Abigail nudged him in the ribs. "It doesn't have wheels. It has *wheel*. One wheel. Can you ride that?"

Andrew just stuck his tongue out at her.

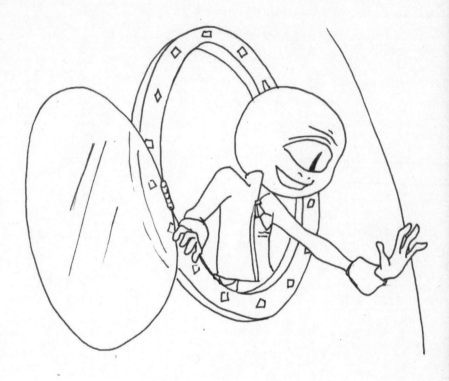

The crowd gasped—*Oooh!*—when a round hatch whisked open on the ship's side. Then they sighed—*Ahhh!*—when they saw that it was a window like the kind on a submarine.

Next, a strange-looking man peered out of the window and waved. He was green, had only one eye, and looked like something from a cheesy old science fiction movie. The heroes didn't know whether to laugh or be afraid.

"Greetings, Earthlings," the green man in the window said slowly. His voice sounded mechanical, like a robot's. "I am Burt. Sure-Burt. From the planet Vanilla Prime. It is my objective to serve you delicious frozen treats."

The crowd shuffled slowly forward, forming a line. Everyone wanted ice cream, but Sure-Burt and his spaceship were a little too convincing. They looked like a real alien and a real spaceship. Their costumes were flawless.

Abigail and Zoë made their way to the front of the line. As usual, Abigail was first.

"Sweet ice cream truck," she told the green man. His ship had to be a truck in disguise, she thought. Everyone knew that aliens and spaceships weren't real.

Sure-Burt scratched his big bald head. "Truck?" he asked, perplexed. "My vehicle is not a truck, Earth-girl. It is a flying saucer."

"You mean it's a U.F.O.," she said, nodding and trying not to smile. She knew how to play along with a joke. She wouldn't give up his secret.

The ice cream man shook his head and laughed. "He. He. He." His voice sounded more robotic than ever.

"I am the U.F.O.," he stated. "Not my ship. See?"

Sure-Burt tapped a triangular patch on the chest of his silver suit. It read, "U.F.O. Sure-Burt. Universal Flavors Officer."

"Your truck is still sweet," Andrew interjected. "And so is your alien costume. Can I order now?"

Sure-Burt blinked slowly before turning to Andrew. Something mysterious flashed in his single eye. Something that made Abigail's spine tingle.

Maybe the man wasn't pretending to be an alien, she worried. Maybe he really was an alien. His mysterious look had been too unfriendly to ignore.

CHAPTER 5:
OUT-OF-THIS WORLD
FLAVORS

"Which flavor do you wish to consume, Earth-ling?" Sure-Burt asked in his mechanical voice. "Please select a treat by name."

With both hands, he pointed at the broad sign of flavors and treats posted on the side of his ship.

The list of ice creams and flavors was like none they had seen before. Cosmic Crunchies and Laserberries? They sounded like snacks for robots, not human foods.

"Asteroids!" Zoë blurted, taking no time to decide. Who knew baby superheroes liked robot food?

Abigail stepped up to the window. She half-expected to see the mysterious look on Sure-Burt's face again. Thankfully, he only smiled.

"I … uh … I'd like a Pickled Saucer Sandwich, please," she said hesitantly. "My baby sister wants Asteroid Zoids."

"And I'll have a Frozen Solar Flare," Andrew added. "Along with two Comet-covered Sundaes for our parents."

That was the rule at home. When the kids got treats from the ice cream truck, so did Mom and Dad. That went for ice cream spaceships, too. It was only fair.

Sure-Burt handed them their treats.

"That will be nine hundred and ninety-nine of your Earth dollars," he announced with a straight face.

Andrew, Abigail, and Zoë's jaws dropped. Nine hundred and ninety-nine dollars! They didn't have that kind of money. It was probably enough to buy a whole ice cream truck. Maybe even an ice cream spaceship.

"And ninety-nine cents," Sure-Burt added.

When the heroes didn't budge, Sure-Burt laughed his robot's laugh.

"He. He. He," he snickered. "I am a U.F.O. An Ultimate Funny Operative. I made a humorous joke."

The heroes and the rest of the crowd breathed a sigh of relief. Then they cheered when Sure-Burt spoke next.

"Today is Out-of-This-World-Savings Day. All ice cream is free. Eat up, Earthlings. Eat as much as you can."

No one noticed the mysterious look return to his face, not even Abigail. Everyone was too interested in ice cream. But the more Sure-Burt served, the darker his look became.

"Eat up, Earthlings," he repeated. "He. He. He."

CHAPTER 6:
VILLANOUS VEGETABLES

Ice cream in hand, the heroes zoomed home as quickly as they could. Even so, Mom met them on the front porch before they took a single lick.

"Put the ice cream in the freezer," she instructed. "It's time for dinner."

"Aww," the heroes complained.

"After?" Zoë asked hopefully.

Mom nodded. "Yes, we'll eat our treats after dinner. For dessert. Now go wash up, and no grumbling."

Even washing up could be fun for our heroes.
They had great imaginations. It was the one super-
power that every kid has.

For Andrew, the soap and water became rac-
ing gloves and the steering wheel of a hot rod.

For Abigail, a pair of boxing gloves.

Even Zoë got into the act. She made herself
look like Santa Claus.

"Ho, ho, ho! It's a T.K.O.!" Abigail exclaimed, dancing around her sister.

The heroes might have played all evening if Dad hadn't called them to dinner. "Who wants ice cream?" he asked.

"Me!" Abigail replied, sprinting to the dinner table.

"Me!" Andrew echoed close behind.

"Applesauce!" Zoë chirped, naming her favorite food.

But there was no applesauce for dinner tonight. The heroes weren't so lucky. Tonight their parents served meat, potatoes, fruit, drinks, and a green nightmare. Broccoli. Yuck! Dinner was ruined. How could their parents be so cruel?

Andrew pushed the food around on his plate. Even with ice cream waiting, he couldn't make himself eat broccoli quickly.

"Are you trying to poison us?" he complained.

"A!" Zoë piped up, and Mom smiled.

"Vitamin A—that's right, Zoë," she agreed. "Broccoli is full of Vitamin A. It's very good for your eyes."

Speaking of eyes, Zoë had a secret weapon. Laser beams. She could fire them from her eyes. When Mom and Dad weren't looking—*Zzzzap!*—her broccoli was vaporized in an instant.

Abigail and Andrew weren't so lucky. They held their noses. They made faces. They did anything they could to force the broccoli down.

When Mom finally announced that it was time for dessert, the heroes cheered. Unfortunately, it would be their last good feeling for quite some time.

Because just then there came a knock on the front door. Answering it would change their lives forever.

CHAPTER 7:
EAT YOUR ICE CREAM

"Last one to the door has alligator breath!" Andrew challenged, leaping to his feet.

The race was on, and you can guess who won—Abigail without breaking a sweat. She just couldn't be beaten in a foot race.

Zoë arrived second and Andrew last. Give him some wheels and the outcome would be different.

"Alligator," Zoë gloated the way only a little sister can.

At the door were the heroes' friends Princess
and Rabbit. Those weren't their real names, of
course, but the nicknames fit.

Rabbit had freckles, big front teeth, and a small
nose that twitched constantly. Princess owned a tri-
cycle as tall as a horse. She rode it proudly around
the neighborhood as if it were a unicorn and she a
real princess. The two were brother and sister.

Today, however, Princess and Rabbit weren't acting like themselves. Princess wasn't riding, and Rabbit's nose wasn't twitching. Something was definitely wrong.

"Eat your ice cream," Princess said. Her voice sounded strange like Sure-Burt's.

"Eat your ice cream," Rabbit repeated in the same robotic voice.

It wasn't just their voices that concerned Abigail. "Look at their eyes!" she cried. "W-what's happened to them?"

Rabbit and Princess tried to push their way into the house. They thrust their desserts forward and continued to chant.

"Eat your ice cream. Eat your ice cream."

Worst of all, their eyes weren't round and colorful anymore. They were as white as vanilla and shaped like tiny ice cream cones.

Thinking fast, Andrew slammed the door before his friends could squeeze inside. Something was wrong with them. Something downright *cold*. They looked hypnotized and were acting crazy about ice cream.

"Let's get Mom and Dad," he said. "They'll know what to do."

Halfway to the kitchen, the heroes spotted their parents. The pair was shuffling clumsily through the house, arms stiff and straight in front of them like zombies. In their cold fingers they clutched Sure-Burt's frosty treats.

"Eat your ice cream," they chanted chillily.

Seeing them, the heroes gasped. Their parents' eyes were shaped like ice cream cones. They had been hypnotized, too!

CHAPTER 8:
THE DEEP BRAIN-FREEZE

Abigail and Andrew knew instantly what had happened. It didn't take superheroes to figure it out. Sure-Burt's ice cream had hypnotized their parents and friends. It had given them the worst brain freezes ever and turned them into zombies! Brain freeze zombies.

"Snap out of it!" Andrew shouted at Mom.

"Wake up!" Abigail tried on Dad.

Nothing worked, and their zombie-parents shuffled closer.

Zoë didn't catch on as quickly as her siblings. She was very young and automatically did whatever her parents asked.

"Eat your ice cream," Mom and Dad said like robots.

So she buzzed over to do just that. To eat her ice cream all gone. She accepted her Asteroid Zoids from Mom and prepared to take a bite.

Abigail saved her. With superhero speed and aim, she snatched a baseball from her duffle bag and threw.

Splack!

The ball struck Zoë's ice cream and knocked it harmlessly from her hand.

"Strike three!" Abigail cheered. "You're outta there!"

"The ice cream is bad, Zoë," Andrew explained. "It's alien ice cream. Anyone who eats it becomes hypnotized."

"They turn into brain-freeze zombies!" Abigail added.

"Automatons!" Zoë gasped, catching on. She knew what mindless zombies were all about.

But knowing didn't help just then. The front door suddenly burst open, and in staggered Rabbit and Princess.

"Eat your ice cream," they said mechanically.

From the other side of the room, Mom and Dad echoed them. "Eat your ice cream."

The heroes were trapped in the middle with nowhere to run.

CHAPTER 9:
ZOMBIES, ZOMBIES EVERYWHERE

There were zombies to the left and zombies to the right. Zombie parents and zombie friends. Our heroes couldn't fight them. The only thing worse would be fighting zombie grandparents.

"Abandon!" Zoë cried, as in abandon ship. She grabbed her siblings by the elbows and started to drag them to safety.

Into the fireplace she dragged them. Over the
logs, up the chimney, and then onto the roof. It was
a daring, narrow escape, but mostly it was messy.

Ploop!

Covered in soot and ash, the heroes burst from the chimney. They were free and away from the zombies. They had traded danger for dirt ... temporarily.

"Nice work, Zoë," Abigail congratulated her sister.

"Astute," Zoë agreed, tapping the side of her head. She could be such a little know-it-all. Most baby sisters could.

"Yeah, good job," Andrew said in a grumpy voice. "Next time try a window."

Abigail shot him a dirty look. Which was easy because she was covered with dirt.

"Isn't it time for your monthly bath?" she teased, plugging her nose.

"Isn't it time for yours?" Andrew retorted, also holding his nose.

Before things really got out of hand, Zoë came to the rescue again. She took a huge gulp of air and then blew her super-breath on her arguing siblings.

Whoo-oo-oosh!

The ash and soot covering them was whisked into the air. So were Abigail and Andrew. They had to grab the chimney to keep from being blown off the roof.

"Whoa, Zoë!" the twins cried together. "That's enough. Stop!"

Zoë snapped her mouth shut, and her siblings crashed back to the roof. They groaned and moaned with discomfort, but their voices were quickly drowned by a familiar sound. It drifted up from below, louder than ever.

"Eat your ice cream," said dozens of robotic voices.

Eat your ice creeaaam

Shoulder to shoulder, the heroes crawled to the edge of the roof. The haunting words weren't coming from their house this time. They were being chanted outdoors.

"Army," Zoë hissed as she peered over the eaves. Next to her Andrew whistled and Abigail gasped.

Their neighborhood was infested with brain-freeze zombies. There really was an army below. Parents, children, and pets stumbled around as if sleepwalking. All of them had hypnotized eyes like tiny ice cream cones.

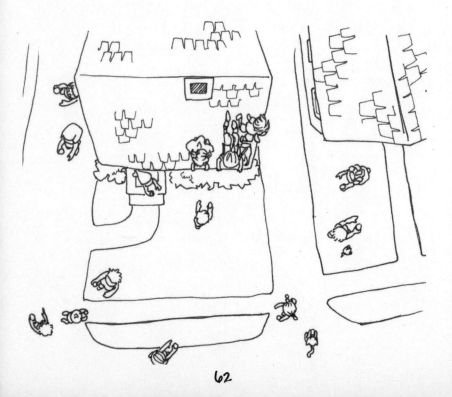

CHAPTER 10:
SPREADING THE FREEZE

"We have to help them," Abigail said fiercely.

Everyone in the neighborhood had been turned into a brain-freeze zombie. There was no telling how many people had eaten Sure-Burt's ice cream.

In fact, Traverse City could be just the beginning. Maybe Cadillac and Petoskey were next. Maybe Lansing, St. Ignace, and Grand Haven were, too. Brain-freeze zombies could overrun Michigan and then the world.

The heroes had to make a stand.

Her brother and sister agreed immediately. Superheroes helped people. That was their job. And right then, a lot of people needed helping.

"We're with you," Andrew said, and Zoë nodded. "Just tell us the plan."

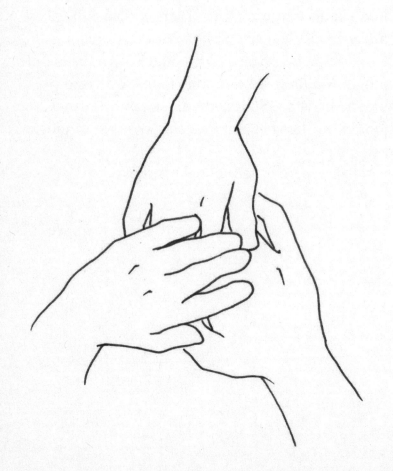

Abigail leaned in close enough to whisper. "I think we should—" she started.

Vvv-rrrooosh!

She never finished. Sure-Burt's spaceship—it was a real spaceship, after all—appeared suddenly on the horizon. From there it streaked toward them like a shooting star.

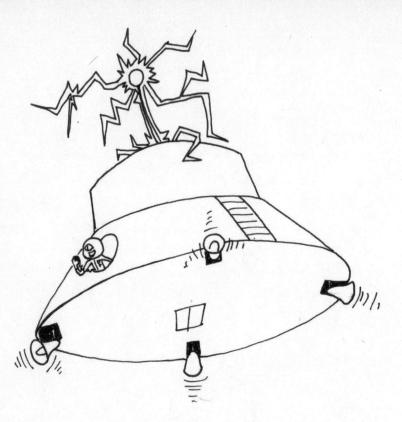

Circus-style music filled the air. It was the ice cream song again. But instead of the words that usually accompanied it, Sure-Burt's mechanical voice blared from loudspeakers on his spaceship.

"Greetings, Earthlings," he droned. "Or should I say Earth-*slaves*? It is time for you to get to work. Come aboard my ship immediately."

So that was his plan, the heroes realized. Sure-Burt hypnotized people and turned them into slaves.

The spaceship landed in the street, and a new line formed. This time, however, the crowd wasn't waiting for ice cream. They were waiting to climb aboard and be whisked away to who-knows-where.

"At least they aren't chanting 'Eat your ice cream' anymore," Andrew muttered. That was something.

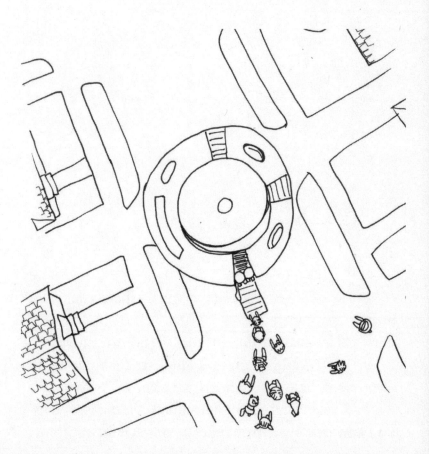

"Okay, we need a new plan," Abigail said in a hurry. "Any ideas?"

"How about the airport?" Andrew suggested eagerly. "I could catch up to that spaceship with an airplane. They have wheels, you know."

"Yeah, yeah," Abigail sighed. "If it has wheels, you can ride it. But we need to get the people off that spaceship, not take them for a ride."

Zoë crossed her eyes and tapped the side of her head again. Older brothers and sisters could be so dense.

"Act," she said simply, and that was her plan—pretend to be zombies. Act like them. Sure-Burt would invite them onto his ship, no questions asked.

Sometimes being a know-it-all baby sister wasn't all bad. Especially when you outsmarted your older siblings.

CHAPTER II:
ROBO-CONE ROBOTS

Arms held stiffly in front of them, the heroes shuffled into the zombie line. Mr. Lee and his dog Stan waited ahead of them. Neither so much as blinked at the super trio. The kids looked just like three more zombies. Nothing to be alarmed about.

The line inched forward slowly but steadily. No one seemed to notice that the heroes weren't really hypnotized.

"So far, so good," Andrew whispered with a wink.

Abigail gritted her teeth. Brothers! she thought. They couldn't keep their mouths shut.

"Eat your ice cream," she responded slowly.

"No pushing," said a metallic voice.

"No shoving," added a second.

On top of the ramp stood a pair of strange-looking robots. They were as tall as the twins and shaped like sugar cones. Their heads were round. They had spoons for arms. And their feet were wrapped in rubber belts like the treads on a toy bulldozer.

"They're robo-cone robots!" Andrew whispered, still unable to keep quiet.

The heroes marched between the pair of robots and into the spaceship. The hatch slammed shut behind them.

Clangk.

Tiny lights blinked on the floor and ceiling. Machinery hummed in the walls. Robo-cone robots scribbled on clipboards, acting important and official.

"Take the Earthlings to the Deep Freeze Cafeteria," a robo-cone ordered. "The boss has special plans for them."

"Not if I can help it," Abigail said softly.

"Shh!" Andrew interjected, thinking it was his turn to keep her quiet.

Zoë cut him short. "Abort," she snapped.

Sisters! Andrew thought. They couldn't keep their mouths shut.

While Andrew grumbled to himself, Abigail quietly pulled a basketball out of her duffle bag and tossed it down a hallway. Its noisy bouncing caught the robots' attention immediately.

"Who goes there?" they demanded. "No pushing. No shoving."

The heroes didn't wait. The ball bounced left, and they ran right. Deep into Sure-Burt's spaceship. Ahead of them lurked danger and the unknown.

CHAPTER 12:
LOST IN SPACE

The spaceship was larger on the inside than it looked on the outside. Crisscrossing hallways, electronic doors, and computers the size of jungle gyms made it a confusing maze.

So when the heroes spotted a porthole that looked to the outside, they stopped for a quick peek.

"Astonishing!" Zoë exclaimed, pointing outside.

Andrew and Abigail agreed with her. The sight through the porthole amazed them. It was also terrifying and hard to believe.

They weren't in Traverse City anymore. They weren't even on Earth. Sure-Burt's spaceship had taken them into outer space.

Planets, stars, asteroids, and even galactic road signs drifted past as the three stared in silence.

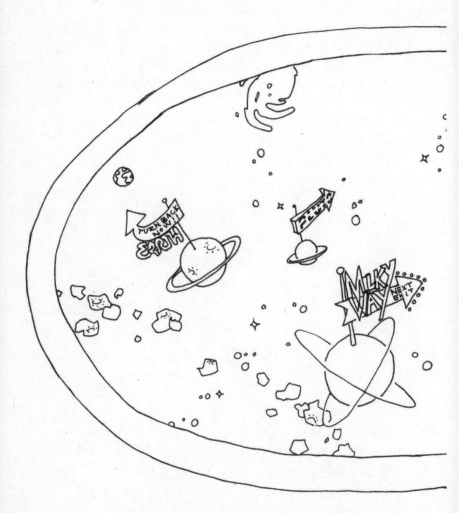

100 LIGHT YEARS

Vanilla
Plume

100 LIGHT YEARS

Finally Andrew spoke. "We have to turn this ship around," he said.

Abigail nodded. "That means we have to find Sure-Burt," she agreed. "He's probably driving."

"And that means it's time for—" Andrew started.

"—Zoë's x-ray vision," Abigail finished.

X-ray vision. Zoë could do that. It was just another one of her superpowers.

First she squinted and held her breath. Then she turned slowly in a circle and stared at the walls.

All the while, her eyes glowed a brighter and brighter blue.

Her brother and sister held their breath, too. Using x-ray vision wasn't as easy as zapping vegetables. Zoë needed to concentrate.

At last she spotted Sure-Burt and pointed a finger forward. The alien was seated in some kind of control room cockpit. He was one corridor away.

"Adversary," she announced, and the twins nodded grimly. The most dangerous part of their rescue mission was about to begin.

CHAPTER 13:
NO EARTHLINGS ALLOWED

Zoë pressed a finger to her lips. Sure-Burt was close, and it was time for sneaking.

She and the twins tiptoed to the control room door. A metal sign hanging there read, "NO EARTH-LINGS ALLOWED."

"This must be the place," Andrew observed.

Surprisingly, Sure-Burt spoke next. His robotic voice came from the other side of the door.

"This is U.F.O. Sure-Burt reporting," he said. "The Earth-slaves are ready for assignment."

A different robotic voice responded a moment later. "Excellent. Take them to Sector Two Percent of the Milky Way. Train them to be milk miners."

"Aye-aye, Commander," Sure-Burt replied. "Over and out."

When Sure-Burt finished talking, Zoë balled her hands into fists. Her face turned red, and the twins stepped backward. They knew what was coming.

"Angry!" Zoë growled.

And to prove that she was, she clobbered the control room door with a super powered right hook.

BLANG!

The door shattered into a million pieces.

Sure-Burt heard the crash and leaped to his feet. Then he spotted the heroes.

"Earthlings!" he gasped. "Why aren't your brains frozen?"

"We don't eat alien ice cream," Abigail snarled as she charged into the control room.

"And we won't be your slaves," Andrew added.

"Not so fast, Earth-brats," Sure-Burt snapped.

Suddenly he held a tub of vanilla in one hand and an ice cream scoop in the other. His arm whirled like a windmill as he scooped and tossed, scooped and tossed. Clump after clump of ice cream hurtled through the air.

"You'll never stop me!" he howled.

And maybe he was right.

CHAPTER 14:
SCOOP DE LOOP

Scoops of ice cream streaked through the control room. They splattered onto instrument panels. They dripped from the ceiling. Anyone but a superhero would have been creamed by now.

But not Abigail. No way. She snatched a tennis racket from her duffle bag and let the scoops have it.

Thwap! She struck with a forehand. *Thwip!* She followed with a backhand. Every scoop that came her way got swatted.

Zoë held her ground too. Vegetables weren't all she could zap. Her lasers blasted vanilla blobs left and right.

Andrew popped out the wheels in his sneakers and skated expertly through Sure-Burt's icy on-
slaught. Because his shoes had wheels, he could
ride them like a downhill skier on a slalom course.
Shh-h-h-whoooh!

Before Sure-Burt could react, Andrew skated past and grabbed the ice cream tub from his green hands.

"Nooo!" the alien wailed.

"It's over, Sure-Burt," Andrew said victoriously.

Sure-Burt's eye narrowed darkly, and he smiled.

"Wrong," he said, chuckling lowly. "It isn't over."

With a flick of his wrist, he raised a small antennae from the top of his ice cream scoop and held the device to his lips. When he spoke next, his words boomed throughout the ship.

The scoop doubled as a microphone!

"Attention robo-cones," Sure-Burt said. "Enact Plan Zero Degrees. Now!"

CHAPTER 15:
PLAN ZERO DEGREES

The heroes held their breath and Sure-Burt laughed. In fact, he laughed so hard that he threw back his head and howled.

"Plan Zero Degrees is my secret weapon," he cackled. "It gives you earthlings permanent brain freezes. You will be my zombies forever!"

Aside from Sure-Burt, only one other thing in the room moved. Not Zoë and not the twins. It was ice cream. Some of it oozed down the walls as it melted. Some plopped from high places and splashed onto the floor.

One clump even dropped into Sure-Burt's gaping mouth as he laughed.

Sploop!

The surprised alien stopped laughing, swallowed, and then blinked twice. His mouth fell open.

"Eat your ice cream," he said, and the heroes cheered.

Sure-Burt had a brain freeze! The ice cream had turned him into a zombie.

"Have a taste of your own medicine, Sure-Burt," Andrew snickered.

"Yeah, game over!" Abigail added.

The twins were feeling pretty proud of themselves. They had defeated a real supervillain.

Only Zoë wasn't celebrating. "Attention," she said seriously.

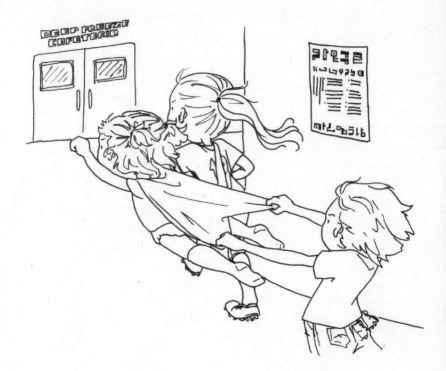

"The others!" Andrew and Abigail exclaimed. Their family and neighbors were still in danger. In their excitement, the twins had forgotten about ominous Plan Zero Degrees.

Abigail sprinted from the control room. Zoë flew close behind. Andrew clutched the end of her cape and held on for dear life. The wheels on his sneakers squealed as she dragged him down the hall.

In the Deep Freeze Cafeteria, the heroes found their friends. The people of Traverse City stood in a crowded lunchroom line. Behind the counter, robo-cone robots served up heaping bowls of alien ice cream.

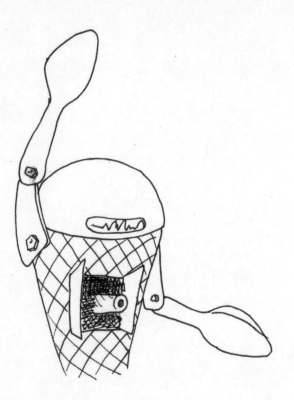

A robo-cone spotted the heroes and raised a spoon-shaped arm.

"Halt, earthlings," it demanded.

Andrew sneered and skated closer. "Halt or what? You going to spoon us to death?"

In response, a panel in the robo-cone's chest slid open. Then a stocky barrel extended from the opening. It looked like the nozzle on an army tank.

"Do not be ridiculous," the robot replied. "We will blast you with our snow cone cannons."

CHAPTER 16:
SNOW CONE CANNONS

Seconds later, a snow cone blizzard howled through the cafeteria. Blue snow cones, red snow cones, purple snow cones, and yellow snow cones filled the air like a swarm of colorful hornets.

Yellow snow cones? The heroes didn't want to know where those came from.

Everything the snow cones struck turned to ice.

Andrew darted right and a lunch table to his left was frozen. Abigail swatted a snow cone and her baseball bat shattered like an icicle.

It took Zoë to get the heroes moving as a team. They didn't have time to play snow cone dodge ball. They needed to stop the robo-cones.

"Attack!" she cried.

Her bat ruined, Abigail reached into her duffle bag. This time she pulled out a bowling ball and sent it spinning into a crowd of robo-cones.

BLARNG!

"Strike!" she cheered. The ball ripped through the robo-cones as if they were bowling pins.

Not wanting to be outdone, Andrew leaned forward and started skating hard. He sped around a group of robo-cones in a blazing circle.

"Watch my Robo-360!" he cheered.

At first the robo-cones tried to keep up. They spun tightly, gears whirling. But Andrew was too fast. In no time, their icy circuits melted and went haywire. Then they fell apart and tumbled to the floor in pieces.

Zoë dismantled the remaining robo-cones with a few quick karate chops. A roundhouse here and an eagle claw there took care of them. The robots didn't know what hit them—again and again and again.

But when the last of the robo-cones fell, a new danger arose. The cafeteria line hadn't slowed, and the people of Traverse City had filled their bowls with more alien ice cream.

Spoons in hand, they faced the heroes.

"Eat your ice cream," they chanted.

CHAPTER 17:
ZOË'S ANTIDOTE

The heroes were too late! They had beaten Sure-Burt and his robot army, but they hadn't prevented their friends and neighbors from eating more ice cream.

For the first time ever, they felt like failures. Plan Zero Degrees had succeeded.

"Now what?" Abigail asked, feeling helpless. "We can't fight ice cream."

Andrew sighed in agreement. "Fire versus water. Summer versus winter. What's the opposite of ice cream?"

Zoë leaped up. "Antidote!" she exclaimed.

Without explaining why, she soared over to the zombified townsfolk.

"Eat your ice cream," they told her, but she ignored them.

She zapped their bowls with a quick blink of her lasers instead. The ice cream inside melted and became a dark liquid. The brains frozen, the townsfolk didn't notice and kept eating.

"Mmm," someone said. "Hot chocolate."

Suddenly the cafeteria echoed with the sounds of slurping and smacking lips. The people of Traverse City were drinking the dark liquid in their bowls like the last bit of soup.

Andrew and Abigail looked at each other in amazement.

"What's the opposite of ice cream?" Andrew asked again.

"Hot chocolate!" he and Abigail answered together.

Hot chocolate! That was Zoë's antidote. It was the opposite of ice cream and cured the zombie brain freeze. Everyone from Traverse City was going to be okay.

"I had the strangest dream," Mom said.

"Where are we?" Rabbit asked, his nose twitching at full speed.

"There's no time to explain," Andrew said. "We have to turn this ship around."

"Hurry, everyone!" Abigail urged. "This way."

Together the heroes and townsfolk raced to the control room. Once they had squeezed inside, Zoë pointed out the ship's big windshield.

"Alien," she said.

Sure-Burt had escaped. He was flying into deep space on a shuttle shaped like a Popsicle. His robotic voice blared over the ship's loudspeakers.

"Farewell, Earthlings," he said. "Your ship is on a crash course with the sun. Have a nice day."

The only sound after that was his laughter.

CHAPTER 18:
HEROES AGAIN

The sun blazed ahead, and the spaceship sped straight toward it. Everyone started to sweat. Some more than others.

"We're doomed!" Rabbit wailed in a panic. Meanwhile, his sister behaved exactly like a spoiled princess by fainting into his arms.

Only the heroes kept calm. Andrew confidently took Sure-Burt's seat at the helm.

"This ship has wheels, right?" he asked.

"Yep," Abigail agreed.

"Aye," Zoë double-agreed.

"Then I can ride it!" Andrew exclaimed. "Hang onto your hats!"

With a whoop, he started pushing buttons, pulling levers, and turning the wheel. The spaceship responded immediately.

Vrrr-ooosh! First it banked left, turning sharply away from the sun. *Zzzz-rooom!* Then it raced full speed ahead.

But before heading home, Andrew zipped around Saturn's rings in a loop-de-loop. What a hotdog!

The joyride came to and end when Andrew expertly landed the spaceship on his family's driveway in Traverse City.

"We'll be the only ones on the street with a spaceship," he said with a grin. Dad just shook his head.

The townsfolk thanked the heroes and then sleepily headed home. They would celebrate tomorrow with a big neighborhood picnic at Bryant Park. Everyone would toast the heroes with cookies and Kool-aid.

"We're very proud of you," Mom and Dad told their children. "But now it's time for bed."

The heroes didn't complain or ask to stay up later. They had saved Traverse City before, and it was no big deal. They would save it again, too, sooner than they knew.

Because that Halloween, a new supervillain would creep from an unlikely place. The heroes needed their sleep to be ready for …

Book #2:
Bowling Over Halloween

Real Heroes Read!

#1: Alien Ice Cream
#2: Bowling Over Halloween
#3: Cherry Bomb Squad
#4: Digging For Dinos
#5: Easter Egg Haunt
#6: Fowl Mouthwash

... and more!

Visit
www.realheroesread.com
for the latest news

Abigail
When it comes to
sports,
she can't be beat

Andrew
If it has wheels,
he can ride it

Baby Zoë
Superhero in a diaper

Also by David Anthony and Charles David

Monsters. Magic. Mystery.

Visit
www.realheroesread.com
to learn more

#1: Cauldron Cooker's Night

#2: Skull in the Birdcage

#3: Early Winter's Orb

#4: Voyage to Silvermight
The Dragonsbane Horn Book One

#5: Trek Through Tanglerout
The Dragonsbane Horn Book Two

#6: Hunt in Hollowdeep
The Dragonsbane Horn Book Three

#7: The Ninespire Experiment

#8: Aware of the Wolf

About the Illustrator
Lys Blakeslee

Lys graduated from Grand Valley State University in Michigan where she pursued a degree in Illustration.

She has always loved to read, and devoted much of her childhood to devouring piles of books from the library.

She spends her summers in Wyoming, MI with her wonderful parents, three younger brothers, two happy cats, and two noisy parakeets.

Broccoli, spinach and ice cream are a few of her favorite foods.

Thank you, Lys!